THE FOLLETT JUST BEGINNING-TO-READ SERIES

The Magic Beans

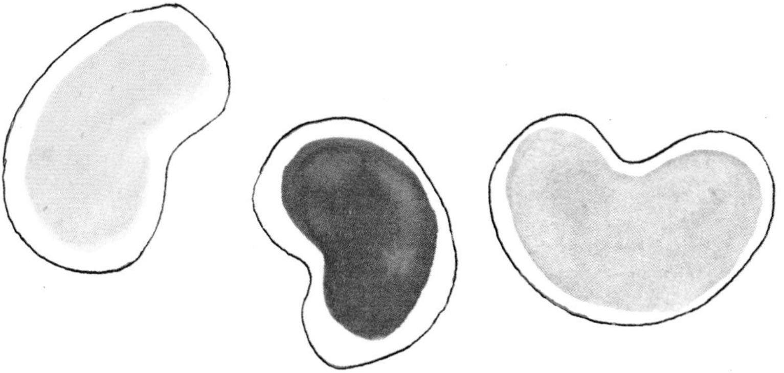

The Magic Beans

Margaret Hillert

Illustrated by Mel Pekarsky

Follett Publishing Company Chicago

Library of Congress Catalog Card Number: AC 66-10514

ISBN 0-695-35483-3 Paper edition
ISBN 0-695-45483-8 Library edition

Fourteenth Printing

Oh, look.

Here is something funny.

One is red.

One is blue.

One is yellow.

One little one.

Two little ones.

Three little ones.

Look, look, look.

Go down here.

Go down in here, little ones.

Oh, oh.

Look and see.

Here is something little.

Up it comes.

Oh, my. Oh, my.

It is big, big, big.

I can go up.

See me go up.

Up, up, up and away.

Look here, look here.

I see a house.

It is a big, big house.

I want to go in.

In I go.

Jump, jump, jump.

It is big in here.

It is big for little me.

Here is something.

It is not big.

It is little and red.

Look, look.

It can work.

It can make something.

Come to me.

Come to me.

I want you.

Come to my house.

Away we go.

Oh, look here.

Here is something for Mother.

Something for my mother.

And here is something.

We can play it.

We can make it play.

It is fun to play.

Come, come.

Come to my house.

Come to my mother.

Here we go.

Away, away, away.

Oh, my.

Here comes something.

Something big.

Where can I go?

Help, help.

Here I go.

Run, run, run.

And here I go.

Down, down, down.

Mother, Mother.

Here I come.

Help me. Help me.

We can work.

We can make it come down.

Here, Mother.

Here is something for you.

Follett JUST Beginning-to-Read Books

Uses of these books. These books are planned for the very youngest readers, those who have been learning to read for about six to eight weeks and who have a small preprimer reading vocabulary. The books are written by Margaret Hillert, a first-grade teacher in the Royal Oak, Michigan, schools. Each book is illustrated in full color.

Children will have a feeling of accomplishment in their first reading experiences with these delightful books that *they can read.*

The Magic Beans

Delightful illustrations accompany this favorite tale of Jack and the Beanstalk which is told in 44 preprimer words.

Word List

7	oh
	look
	here
	is
	something
	funny
	one
	red
	blue
	yellow
8	little
	two
	three
9	go
	down
	in
10	and
	see
	up
	it
	comes
11	my
	big
12	I
	can
	me
	away
13	a
	house
14	want
	to
	jump
15	for
16	not
17	work
	make
18	you
	we
19	mother
20	play
	fun
23	where
24	help
	run